THE STORY OF
BIP
written and illustrated by
MARCEL MARCEAU

HARPER & ROW, PUBLISHERS
New York · Evanston · San Francisco · London

To all the people of the earth
and to all those who are still
children at heart.

Do you know Bip? I know him very well.
He was born in a beautiful French city called Paris.
Here is Bip—with the pale face, wearing a top hat
on which a red flower is trembling. Bip—that
moonlike figure leaning against the gas streetlamp
yellowed by time. Bip—*c'est moi.*

I had always dreamed of being a magician, and on this particular night
I was dreaming of it more than usual. Suddenly I felt wings growing from
my shoulders. I rose from the ground, and I began to fly above the rooftops.
  Soaring higher and higher, I flew through the clouds, and I saw
beneath me the earth, the rivers, the valleys. Even the mountains looked
like tiny anthills. I swept above the seas and storms.

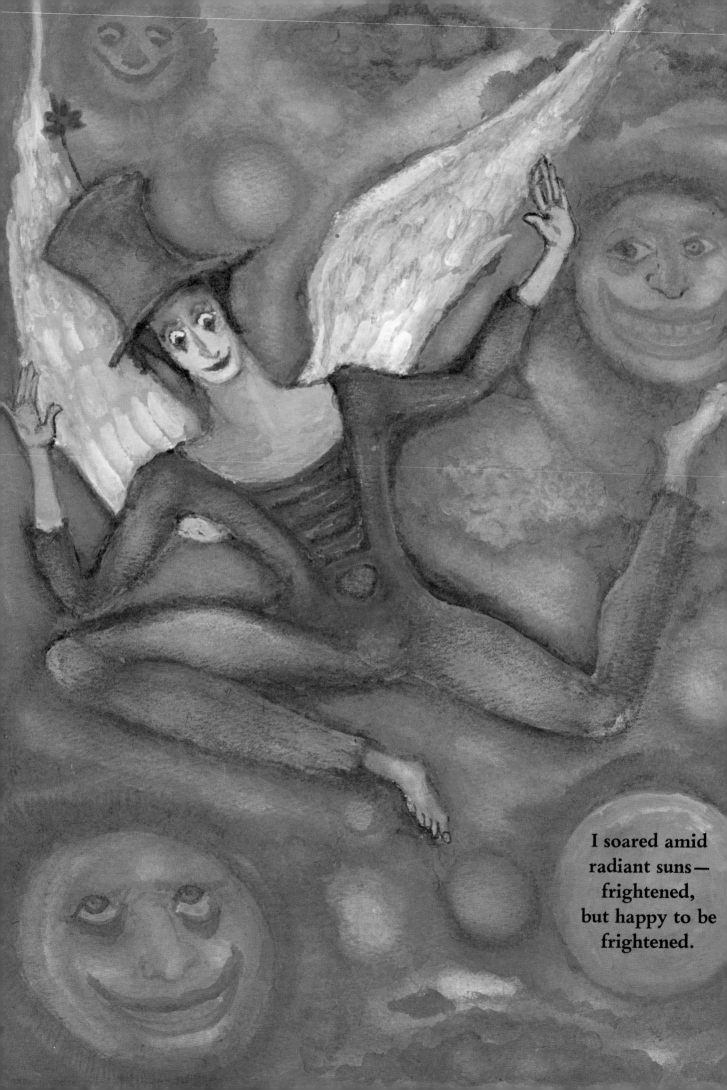

I soared amid
radiant suns—
frightened,
but happy to be
frightened.

Suddenly night began to fall. I saw multitudes of stars, and among them the earth looked like a gem of burning blue. I felt far from human beings, far from all the things I had loved, far from that life in which I had laughed and cried. I had become an angel.

Daylight returned. The stars faded
in the sky. The moon became so
pale that I could no longer see
it. I felt myself being drawn
dangerously close to the sun,
as a moth toward a flame.
In the rays of the golden
sun one of my wings
began to burn. Then
the second one also.
I wanted to cry,
but an angel
has no tears.

I fell through space, my wings on fire, and
landed on a world where I did not recognize
the foliage, or the atmosphere, or the time.
Was I living in a beautiful dream? I saw
phantasmagoric landscapes, fantastic shadows,
colors of another world. How long did I remain
here? I felt lonely in the middle of this strange
beauty. I wanted to share my feelings with
other people. I longed to see men and women
and children. I longed to tell them about this
world. But I no longer had my wings. They
had burned in the rays of the great sun.

Lifting my eyes to the sky,
I asked help of the moon. But
the moon answered, "Look to the earth
for help. You *are* on the moon." I wanted
to feel a tear running down my white cheek.
I wanted to feel the beating of my heart. But I had no
more heart, no more body, no more tears. I had become a spirit.

And then I saw Bip, hovering gently in space. At first I was
frightened, but then I thought, *This is nothing to fear. After all, I am
his spirit.* "Hey, just a minute! Wait for me!" And I rose into the atmosphere
without wings and grabbed hold of Bip's shoulders. I entered my body again
and at once felt my heart beating.

Then I longed to return to earth. I fought my way through
magnetic storms. Lightning flashed continuously around me. I was
tossed like a blind bird. I thought, *Bip, this is the end of everything.*

Suddenly all
was quiet again.
Gliding slowly
toward the earth,
I landed in the top
of a giant tree.
Looking upon my
familiar earth, I
slid down the
trunk of the tree
to the ground.

There was a small
pond, and I saw Bip's
pale face and red lips
reflected in the water.
Tears ran down
my cheeks. Here I was,
a living being among
the millions of souls
who fill the earth.

I left the countryside and walked through a town.
There I saw people —from everywhere. Before this,
I had lived in my own little world; but now I wanted
to tell the people of my discovery. I was part of
the universe —of the millions of stars and planets, part of
the sky and the moon and the sun, part of *them*, the people
of the earth. And I wanted to tell them that although
there was violence, ugliness, and cruelty in our world,
there also could be harmony, love, and peace.

Human life was like a growing tree in a beautiful garden. I wanted to cry out my joy, but my voice was silent. I smiled at the people; they smiled back.

I ran from the town back to the fields. I drank
the water. I kissed the earth, began to run.
I picked flowers and imitated the flight of birds,
longing to offer a huge flower to the world.

Back on the road, I felt under my feet millions of cars
riding silently. The air was filled with music.
I could not see where it came from. I looked all around me.
Down a white road, there was a black dot on the horizon.
I began to run faster and faster, drawn toward the dot
as if it were a magnet.

Now I could hear beautiful music which sounded like
a symphony of birds. The small dot had become a giant circus
tent, and I heard a roar of laughter from within. It surged toward
me like the waves that swell the sea. I touched the canvas
of the tent. My heart was pounding. A big drum was rolling.

As I entered the center of the ring, thousands of eyes
riveted upon me. How could I speak to them without words?
Slowly my body—legs and arms, hands and feet, my face,
my soul—began to move in silent outcry.
And with an enormous gesture, I caressed the empty air
and embraced the world.